Clarice Lispector
Love

Tr. Katrina Dodson

ERIS
gems

A LITTLE TIRED, THE GROCERIES stretching out her new knit sack, Ana boarded the tram. She placed the bundle in her lap and the tram began to move. She then settled back in her seat trying to get comfortable, with a half-contented sigh.

Ana's children were good, something true and succulent. They were growing up, taking their baths, demanding for themselves, misbehaved, ever more complete moments. The kitchen was after all spacious, the faulty stove gave off small explosions. The heat was stifling in the apartment they were paying off bit by bit. But the wind whipping the curtains she herself had cut to measure reminded her that if she wanted she could stop and wipe her brow, gazing at the calm horizon. Like a farmhand. She had sown the seeds she had in her hand, no others, but these alone. And trees were growing. Her brief conversation with the electric bill collector was growing, the water in the laundry sink was growing, her children were growing, the table with food was growing, her husband coming home with the newspapers and smiling with hunger, the tiresome singing of the maids in the building. Ana gave to everything, tranquilly, her small, strong hand, her stream of life.

A certain hour of the afternoon was more dangerous. A certain hour of the afternoon the trees she had planted would laugh at her. When nothing else needed her strength, she got worried. Yet she felt more solid than ever, her body had filled out a bit and it was a sight to see her cut the fabric for the boys' shirts, the large scissors snapping on the cloth. All her vaguely artistic desire had long since been directed toward making the days fulfilled and beautiful; over time, her taste for the decorative had developed and supplanted her inner disorder. She seemed to have discovered that everything could be perfected, to each thing she could lend a harmonious appearance; life could be wrought by the hand of man.

Deep down, Ana had always needed to feel the firm root of things. And this is what a home bewilderingly had given her. Through winding paths, she had fallen into a woman's fate, with the surprise of fitting into it as if she had invented it. The man she'd married was a real man, the children she'd had were real children. Her former youth seemed as strange to her as one of life's illnesses. She had gradually emerged from it to discover that one could also live without happiness: abolishing it, she had found a legion of people, previously invisible, who lived the way a person works—with persistence, continuity, joy. What had happened to Ana before she had a home was forever out of reach: a restless exaltation so often mistaken for unbearable happiness. In exchange she had created something at last comprehensible, an adult life. That was what she had wanted and chosen.

The only thing she worried about was being careful during that dangerous hour of the afternoon, when the house was empty and needed nothing more from her, the sun high, the family members scattered to their duties. As she looked at the clean furniture, her heart would contract slightly in astonishment. But there was no room in her life for feeling tender toward her astonishment—she'd smother it with the same skill the household chores had given her. Then she'd go do the shopping or get something repaired, caring for her home and family in their absence. When she returned it would be the end of the afternoon and the children home from school needed her. In this way night would fall, with its peaceful vibration. In the morning she'd awake haloed by her calm duties. She'd find the furniture dusty and dirty again, as if repentantly come home. As for herself, she obscurely participated in the gentle black roots of the world. And nourished life anonymously. That was what she had wanted and chosen.

The tram went swaying along the tracks, heading down broad avenues. Soon a more humid breeze blew announcing, more than the end of the afternoon, the end of the unstable hour. Ana breathed deeply and a great acceptance gave her face a womanly air.

The tram would slow, then come to a halt. There was time to relax before Humaitá. That was when she looked at the man standing at the tram stop.

The difference between him and the others was that he really was stopped. Standing there, his hands reaching in front of him. He was blind.

What else could have made Ana sit up warily? Something uneasy was happening. Then she saw: the blind man was chewing gum... A blind man was chewing gum.

Ana still had a second to think about how her brothers were coming for dinner—her heart beat violently, at intervals. Leaning forward, she stared intently at the blind man, the way we stare at things that don't see us. He was chewing gum in the dark. Without suffering, eyes open. The chewing motion made it look like he was smiling and then suddenly not smiling, smiling and not smiling—as if he had insulted her, Ana stared at him. And whoever saw her would have the impression of a woman filled with hatred. But she kept staring at him, leaning further and further forward—the tram suddenly lurched throwing her unexpectedly backward, the heavy knit sack tumbled from her lap, crashed to the floor—Ana screamed, the conductor gave the order to stop before he knew what was happening—the tram ground to a halt, the passengers looked around frightened.

Unable to move to pick up her groceries, Ana sat up, pale. A facial expression, long unused, had reemerged with difficulty, still tentative, incomprehensible. The paperboy laughed while returning her bundle. But the eggs had broken inside their newspaper wrapping. Viscous, yellow yolks dripped through the mesh. The blind man had interrupted his chewing and was reaching out his uncertain hands, trying in vain to grasp what was happening. The package of eggs had been thrown from the bag and, amid the passengers' smiles and the conductor's signal, the tram lurched back into motion.

A few seconds later nobody was looking at her. The tram rumbled along the tracks and the blind man chewing gum stayed behind forever. But the damage was done.

The knit mesh was rough between her fingers, not intimate as when she had knit it. The mesh had lost its meaning and being on a tram was a snapped thread; she didn't know what to do with the groceries on her lap. And like a strange song, the world started up again all around. The damage was done. Why? could she have forgotten there were blind people? Compassion was suffocating her, Ana breathed heavily. Even the things that existed before this event were now wary, had a more hostile, perishable aspect... The world had become once again a distress. Several years were crashing down, the yellow yolks were running. Expelled from her own days, it seemed to her that the people on the street were in peril, kept afloat on the surface of the darkness by a minimal balance—and for a moment the lack of meaning left them so free they didn't know where to go. The perception of an absence of law happened so suddenly that Ana clutched the seat in front of her, as if she might fall off the tram, as if things could be reverted with the same calm they no longer held.

What she called a crisis had finally come. And its sign was the intense pleasure with which she now looked at things, suffering in alarm. The heat had become more stifling, everything had gained strength and louder voices. On the Rua Voluntários da Pátria a revolution seemed about to break out, the sewer grates were dry, the air dusty. A blind man chewing gum had plunged the world into dark voraciousness. In every strong person there was an absence of compassion for the blind man and people frightened her with the vigor they possessed. Next to her was a lady in blue, with a face. She averted her gaze, quickly. On the sidewalk, a woman shoved her son! Two lovers interlaced their fingers smiling... And the blind man? Ana had fallen into an excruciating benevolence.

She had pacified life so well, taken such care for it not to explode. She had kept it all in serene comprehension, separated each person from the rest, clothes were clearly made to be worn and you could choose the evening movie from the newspaper—everything wrought in such a way that one day followed another. And a blind man chewing gum was shattering it all to pieces. And through this compassion there appeared to Ana a life full of sweet nausea, rising to her mouth.

Only then did she realize she was long past her stop. In her weak state everything was hitting her with a jolt; she left the tram weak in the knees, looked around, clutching the eggstained mesh. For a moment she couldn't get her bearings. She seemed to have stepped off into the middle of the night.

It was a long street, with high, yellow walls. Her heart pounding with fear, she sought in vain to recognize her surroundings, while the life she had discovered kept pulsating and a warmer, more mysterious wind whirled round her face. She stood there looking at the wall. At last she figured out where she was. Walking a little further along a hedge, she passed through the gates of the Botanical Garden.

She trudged down the central promenade, between the coconut palms. There was no one in the Garden. She put her packages on the ground, sat on a bench along a path and stayed there a long while.

The vastness seemed to calm her, the silence regulated her breathing. She was falling asleep inside herself.

From a distance she saw the avenue of palms where the afternoon was bright and full. But the shade of the branches covered the path.

All around were serene noises, scent of trees, little surprises among the vines. The whole Garden crushed by the ever faster instants of the afternoon. From where did that half-dream come that encircled her? Like a droning of bees and birds. Everything was strange, too gentle, too big.

A light, intimate movement startled her—she spun around. Nothing seemed to have moved. But motionless in the central avenue stood a powerful cat. Its fur was soft. Resuming its silent walk, it disappeared.

Worried, she looked around. The branches were swaying, the shadows wavering on the ground. A sparrow was pecking at the dirt. And suddenly, in distress, she seemed to have fallen into an ambush. There was a secret labor underway in the Garden that she was starting to perceive.

In the trees the fruits were black, sweet like honey. On the ground were dried pits full of circumvolutions, like little rotting brains. The bench was stained with purple juices. With intense gentleness the waters murmured. Clinging to the tree trunk were the luxuriant limbs of a spider. The cruelty of the world was tranquil. The murder was deep. And death was not what we thought.

While imaginary—it was a world to sink one's teeth into, a world of voluminous dahlias and tulips. The trunks were crisscrossed by leafy parasites, their embrace was soft, sticky. Like the revulsion that precedes a surrender—it was fascinating, the woman was nauseated, and it was fascinating.

The trees were laden, the world was so rich it was rotting. When Ana thought how there were children and grown men going hungry, the nausea rose to her throat, as if she were pregnant and abandoned. The moral of the Garden was something else. Now that the blind man had led her to it, she trembled upon the first steps of a sparkling, shadowy world, where giant water lilies floated monstrous. The little flowers scattered through the grass didn't look yellow or rosy to her, but the color of bad gold and scarlet. The decomposition was deep, perfumed... But all the heavy things, she saw with her head encircled by a swarm of insects, sent by the most exquisite life in the world. The breeze insinuated itself among the flowers. Ana sensed rather than smelled its sweetish scent... The Garden was so pretty that she was afraid of Hell.

It was nearly evening now and everything seemed full, heavy, a squirrel leaped in the shadows. Beneath her feet the earth was soft, Ana inhaled it with delight. It was fascinating, and she felt nauseated.

But when she remembered the children, toward whom she was now guilty, she stood with a cry of pain. She grabbed her bag, went down the dark path, reached the promenade. She was nearly running—and she saw the Garden all around, with its haughty impersonality. She rattled the locked gates, rattled them gripping the rough wood. The guard appeared, shocked not to have seen her.

Until she reached the door of her building, she seemed on the verge of a disaster. She ran to the elevator clutching the mesh sack, her soul pounding in her chest—what was happening? Her compassion for the blind man was as violent as an agony, but the world seemed to be hers, dirty, perishable, hers. She opened her front door. The living room was large, square, the doorknobs were gleaming spotlessly, the windowpanes gleaming, the lamp gleaming—what new land was this? And for an instant the wholesome life she had led up till now seemed like a morally insane way to live. The boy who ran to her was a being with long legs and a face just like hers, who ran up and hugged her. She clutched him tightly, in alarm. She protected herself trembling. Because life was in peril. She loved the world, loved what had been created—she loved with nausea. The same way she'd always been fascinated by oysters, with that vaguely sick feeling she always got when nearing the truth, warning her. She embraced her son, nearly to the point of hurting him. As if she had learned of an evil—the blind man or the lovely Botanical Garden?—she clung to him, whom she loved more than anything. She had been touched by the demon of faith. Life is horrible, she said to him softly, ravenous. What would she do if she heeded the call of the blind man? She would go alone... There were places poor and rich that needed her. She needed them... I'm scared, she said. She felt the child's delicate ribs between her arms, heard his frightened sobbing. Mama, the boy called. She held him away from her, looked at that face, her heart cringed. Don't let Mama forget you, she told him. As soon as the child felt her embrace loosen, he broke free and fled to the bedroom door, looking at her from greater safety. It was the worst look she had ever received. The blood rushed to her face, warming it.

She let herself fall into a chair, her fingers still gripping the mesh sack. What was she ashamed of?

There was no escape. The days she had forged had ruptured the crust and the water was pouring out. She was facing the oyster. And there was no way not to look at it. What was she ashamed of? That it was no longer compassion, it wasn't just compassion: her heart had filled with the worst desire to live.

She no longer knew whether she was on the side of the blind man or the dense plants. The man had gradually receded into the distance and in torture she seemed to have gone over to the side of whoever had wounded his eyes. The Botanical Garden, tranquil and tall, was revealing this to her. In horror she was discovering that she belonged to the strong part of the world—and what name should she give her violent mercy? She would have to kiss the leper, since she would never be just his sister. A blind man led me to the worst in myself, she thought in alarm. She felt banished because no pauper would drink water from her ardent hands. Ah! it was easier to be a saint than a person! By God, hadn't it been real, the compassion that had fathomed the deepest waters of her heart? But it was the compassion of a lion.

Humiliated, she knew the blind man would prefer a poorer love. And, trembling, she also knew why. The life of the Botanical Garden was calling her as a werewolf is called by the moonlight. Oh! but she loved the blind man! she thought with moist eyes. Yet this wasn't the feeling you'd go to church with. I'm scared, she said alone in the living room. She got up and went to the kitchen to help the maid with dinner.

But life made her shiver, like a chill. She heard the school bell, distant and constant. The little horror of the dust threading together the underside of the oven, where she discovered the little spider. Carrying the vase to change its water—there was the horror of the flower surrendering languid and sickening to her hands. The same secret labor was underway there in the kitchen. Near the trash can, she crushed the ant with her foot. The little murder of the ant. The tiny body trembled. The water droplets were dripping into the stagnant water in the laundry sink. The summer beetles. The horror of the inexpressive beetles. All around was a silent, slow, persistent life. Horror, horror. She paced back and forth across the kitchen, slicing the steaks, stirring the sauce. Round her head, circling, round the light, the mosquitoes of a sweltering night. A night on which compassion was raw as bad love. Between her two breasts sweat slid down. Faith was breaking her, the heat of the stove stung her eyes.

Then her husband arrived, her brothers and their wives arrived, her brothers' children arrived.

They ate dinner with all the windows open, on the ninth floor. An airplane went shuddering past, threatening in the heat of the sky. Though made with few eggs, the dinner was good. Her children stayed up too, playing on the rug with the others. It was summer, it would be pointless to send them to bed. Ana was a little pale and laughed softly with the others.

After dinner, at last, the first cooler breeze came in through the windows. They sat around the table, the family. Worn out from the day, glad not to disagree, so ready not to find fault. They laughed at everything, with kind and human hearts.

The children were growing up admirably around them. And as if it were a butterfly, Ana caught the instant between her fingers before it was never hers again.

Later, when everyone had gone and the children were already in bed, she was a brute woman looking out the window. The city was asleep and hot. Would whatever the blind man had unleashed fit into her days? How many years would it take for her to grow old again? The slightest movement and she'd trample one of the children. But with a lover's mischief, she seemed to accept that out of the flower emerged the mosquito, that the giant water lilies floated on the darkness of the lake. The blind man dangled among the fruits of the Botanical Garden.

If that was the oven exploding, the whole house would already be on fire! she thought rushing into the kitchen and finding her husband in front of the spilled coffee.

"What happened?!" she screamed vibrating all over.

He jumped at his wife's fright. And suddenly laughed in comprehension:

"It was nothing," he said, "I'm just clumsy." He looked tired, bags under his eyes.

But encountering Ana's strange face, he peered at her with greater attention. Then he drew her close, in a swift caress.

"I don't want anything to happen to you, ever!" she said.

"At least let the oven explode at me," he answered smiling.

She stayed limp in his arms. This afternoon something tranquil had burst, and a humorous, sad tone was hanging over the house. "Time for bed," he said, "it's late." In a gesture that wasn't his, but that seemed natural, he held his wife's hand, taking her along without looking back, removing her from the danger of living.

The dizziness of benevolence was over.

And, if she had passed through love and its hell, she was now combing her hair before the mirror, for an instant with no world at all in her heart. Before going to bed, as if putting out a candle, she blew out the little flame of the day.

ERIS

265 Riverside Dr.
New York, NY 10025

Clarice Lispector, "Love (Amor)", translated by Katrina Dodson, excerpted from *The Complete Stories* (New Directions, 2015).

ISBN 978-1-971559-26-1

eris.press